BEGAT

BY

THOMAS ALEXANDER

Begat by Thomas Alexander

Direct Light Publishing
45 Dudley Court, Endell Street, London, WC2H 9RF

Permissions may be sought directly from:
Publishing Rights Department, 45 Dudley Court, Endell Street, London, WC2H 9RF
Email: info@directlight-publications.com
Library of Congress Cataloguing in Publication Data
Application submitted.
British Library Cataloguing in Publication Data
Application submitted.
04 05 06 07 08 09 10 9 8 7 6 5 4 3 2
uuid:6452fce2-cd8b-440b-8205-8a7a1a32ea04
ISBN: 978-1-941979-00-6

–

Edited by Shirin Laghai for Direct Light Publications.

Available in Epub and Soft Cover from Direct Light
EPUB ISBN: 978-1-941979-01-3

Cover design by SimplyA
© 2014 simplya@directlight-publications.com

I

for Shirin
Who this heart was for.

ABOUT THE AUTHOR

Thomas Alexander has worked in almost all forms of theatre, from opera to children's performances, working as everything from stage hand to costume designer, and has seen his work translated into four different languages and performed as far afield as America and Afghanistan.

His plays; *Writing William, Begat, Great & The Visitor* along with his novel; *A Scattering Of Orphans* have been published by DIRECT LIGHT PUBLICATIONS.

Also by the Author

PLAYS

Happiness
Murder Me Gently
The Family
Begat
The Crossroads Country
Great
The Visitor
When Dusk Brings Glory
The Recruitment Officer
Writer's Block
The Last Christmas
Writing William
The Big Match

ONE ACT PLAYS

Four Widows and A Funeral
For Arts Sake
The TV
Life TM
The Dance

ADAPTATIONS
William Shakespeare's' R3
Othello

NOVELS

A Scattering Of Orphans

BEGAT

BY

THOMAS ALEXANDER

IN A COUNTRY, AFTER THE WAR,

A JUDGE THROWS A DINNER PARTY, SEEKING SUPPORT AGAINST A POWERFUL MINISTER WHO HAS RAPED AND KILLED A SERVANT GIRL.

BUT THE JUDGE HIMSELF IS THE TARGET TONIGHT, AND THE SHADOW OF THE WAR HE SO DESPERATELY WANTS TO LEAVE BEHIND THREATENS TO ENGULF HIS FAMILY AS A YOUNG WOMAN SEEKS REVENGE FOR THE SINS OF HIS PAST.

FOREWORD

by Thomas Alexander

One of the first things all students of psychology learn is that relativity isn't only connected to the passage of time.

They don't phrase it like this, of course, but the concept of memory – a module taught to every school student in Psych 101 – is not just the bedrock of the subject, it's also the way we view the world and, more importantly, ourselves.

Reality is what we think happened, not what actually has.

There has been, over the years, numerous studies into false memory syndrome. From child abuse cases to death row inmates, the idea of false memories, implanted or otherwise, has gained world-wide attention and for good reason.

Tricks and exploitations, everything from colours and content to smells and sound, have long been used in advertising to help us associate with products. Pictures of seaside family holidays, the use of pastel shades, or shaping a mall like a church are all selected by advertisers to help stimulate positive memories, real or imagined, and use them to persuade us to buy their products. But it goes a lot further than that.

The human brain has been shown to be incredibly manipulative. Indeed, recent studies have suggested that the brain evolved in such a way in order to replace reality, with all its perils and pit stops, with delusion to protect the positivity of the individual, allowing us to go on and accomplish feats which no sane or objective person would think of doing, like building skyscrapers or watching reality TV.

Whether that's true or not, what is beyond doubt is that humans can be influenced into holding memory through suggestion, both post and pre event, by something as simple as a colour, a word, or a scent. What we remember is subject to how we felt, how we see the world, and whether or not we've seen too many episodes of detective dramas on television.

As any policeman will tell you, given enough witnesses someone will claim that a monkey was driving and that the man he hit was, in fact, their long lost grandfather who has been dead these last ten years.

This, of course, is not news to the dramatist. From Rashomon onward, the writer has long seen great scope in attacking the concepts of truth and relativity, and none so much as the playwright.

When I started writing Begat, however, it wasn't with this central premise in mind, but as I continued one of the things that struck me was that almost all of the characters seemed to disagree with each other over the events leading up to the play. Another example, if you will, of writers having the most relative minds of all

– even their own fictional characters are open to suggestion!

The central premise that I wanted to write about was the concept of justice when meted out by differing value systems, but I'm not at all sure that this is still the core concept of the story for me.

There are many despicable crimes committed in the play in the name of justice – usually, much like in life, against women and I apologise for that – from rape to being burnt alive, but the only one that is without a doubt not committed with justice in mind is the only one that goes unpunished.

The Begat in the title is in correlation to that and perhaps is still the central motif, but one of the things that stood out for me early on was how the characters existed inside their own realities, with their own subjective memories of events in almost complete opposition to the memories of those around them.

This comes to the fore in the death of Diarmen, the bodyguard (or lost love, depending on perspective), which is left almost completely unexplained in terms of events. Other characters posit ideas for his death, but there is nothing to prove whether their contradictory views are true or not. We are simply left to hope that the actor has reason enough to convey it convincingly within a back-story of his own creation. If I were to venture a direction, I would urge them to look toward the title, but it is not the writer's place to deal with such things.

I wrote this play on a Blackberry tablet in Melbourne in the summer of 2012, and I am indebted to the State Library for its austerity and Shirin Laghai for her lack of it.

Without either it wouldn't have been possible.

A final word: As much as possible, I have tried to leave the religions and nationalities up to the audience's imagination. There are some traits that clearly implicate certain perceptions on the matter of justice, but I hope I have created enough contradictions to eliminate any such accusations. This is not a polemic. It is neither for nor against any sect or section of society. It is a story of competing theories of justice, and how they can create and maintain hatred and injustice. It is a tale of subjective viewpoints. And it is a play about how we are ever and always seeking the facts of events in a world where none actually exists.

Thomas Alexander - London 2014

BEGAT

Cast of Characters

AUTHORS NOTE

The cast is specifically designed so that a number of roles can be doubled. A cast of 5-6 is more than adequate.

SENUR – Mid Twenties./ Accented

KARS - Early Twenties.

JUDGE – Sixties. Rich.

DIARMEN – Bodyguard. Physical. Forties

DOCTOR – Sixties. Rich.

OLD – Male. Sixties. Poor.

YOUNG – Male. Twenties. Poor.

KIFUR – Forties Poor. Accented

ANISI – Twenties/Early Thirties. Poor

SENATOR – Sixties./ Rich.

YOUNG SENUR – A child. No more than ten

ANNOUNCER

SARAH (non speaking) Forties.

BEGAT

ACT 1

ACT 1

SCENE 1

CURTAINS.

A MAN IN A WHITE SUIT STEPS FORWARD, WELCOMING GUESTS TO A LAVISH PARTY AT THE HOME OF THE JUDGE.

ANNOUNCER Congressman Taimor and Ms Senur Kafii.

LIGHTS UP ON THE HACIENDA.

A BALCONY STRETCHING HIGH OVER THE DEEP ARCHES OF THE BUILDING LOOKS OUT ON THE VAST LAWNS OF THE PRESTIGIOUS PROPERTY.

CICADAS SING FROM HIGH TREES, A CACOPH-ONY DROWNING OUT A DISTANT QUARTET SOMEWHERE IN THE BUILDING IN THE MIDST OF THE PARTY.

ON THE BALCONY A YOUNG WOMAN STANDS LOOKING OUT. THE NIGHT IS HOT AND HU-MID. SHE IS DRESSED IN A SIMPLE SLIP OF A DRESS. A SCARF, WORN FOR PROPRIETY, HAS SLIPPED OFF HER SHOULDERS AND HANGS FROM HER ARMS AROUND HER WAIST IN THE HEAT.

SHE IS PRETTY IN AN UNCONVENTIONAL WAY,

DARK AND EARTHY. SHE SEEMS AT PEACE.

KARS STEPS OUT ONTO THE BALCONY, TWO GLASSES OF CHAMPAGNE IN HIS HAND. HE IS WELL DRESSED IN FINE COTTON AND LEATHER SHOES, HIS HAIR PULLED BACK. YOUTH AND BEAUTY ARE ON HIS SIDE.

HE APPROACHES HER CALMLY AND HANDS HER ONE OF THE GLASSES. PAUSING SHE TAKES IT WITHOUT A WORD, AND THE PAIR OF THEM LOOK OUT INTO THE NIGHT SKY.

KARS   I liked what you said. In there.

SENUR   What did I say?

KARS   The murder. People should speak out like that more often.

SENUR   I don't think I made many friends.

KARS   And is that what you want – friends?

SENUR   We all need friends.

PAUSE.

KARS   He did it. Of course. We all know that, the bloated... Did you ever meet him? The senator?

SENUR   Is that what you came out to talk to me about?

KARS   Perhaps.

SENUR   Thank you for the champagne.

KARS   Who did you come with?

SENUR   Who said I came with anyone.

KARS   This doesn't look like your sort of party.

SENUR   Whose party is it?

KARS   Mine.

SENUR   Then it doesn't look like my kind of party. What do you imagine my sort of party would look like anyway?

KARS   Better.

SHE SMILES.

SENUR   Do you always come to your father's parties?

KARS   I have to. I live here. It's my home.

SENUR   I see.

KARS   Do you?

SHE LEANS IN AND KISSES HIM.

SENUR   Very.

HE LOOKS AT HER FOR A SECOND AND THEN REACHING OUT PULLS HER PASSIONATELY TOWARDS HIM. SHE RESPONDS, PULLING HIM IN DEEPER, THEN BITING HIS LIP STEPS BACK QUICKLY.

HE LOOKS AT HER, PAIN MAKING HIM ATTEND TO HIS LIP.

HE GLARES AT HER AND THEN, THROWING HIS GLASS AGAINST THE WALL, RUSHES INTO HER, CRUSHING HIMSELF AGAINST HER.

SHE LETS HER GLASS FALL TO THE FLOOR AND RESPONDS, THEIR PASSION RISING, GREEDY WITH EACH OTHER.

AT THE LAST MOMENT HE TURNS HER SO

THAT SHE FACES OUT FROM THE BALCONY AND, LIFTING HER DRESS TO FIND NO UNDER-WEAR, ENTERS HER.

AS SOON AS SHE IS AWAY FROM HIM HER FACE CHANGES FROM PASSION TO ENDURANCE.

KARS   God!

HE FINISHES, COLLAPSING ONTO HER BACK. SHE STROKES HIS HAIR.

SENUR   It's alright.

SOMETHING IS STICKING INTO HIM, SOME-THING ATTACHED TO THE BACK OF HER DRESS. HE ADJUSTS HIMSELF AND REACHES FOR IT.

FINDING A SMALL GUN SECRETED THERE HE PULLS AWAY FROM HER.

KARS   What's this?

HE IS STRUGGLING, ADJUSTING HIMSELF AND TRYING TO DRESS, ALL THE WHILE LOOKING AT THE GUN.

SHE IS CALM AND QUIET. SHE TAKES A STEP TOWARDS HIM. HE POINTS THE GUN AT HER.

KARS (cont) No!

SHE STOPS, RADIATING CALM, AND WAITS FOR HIM TO SPEAK AGAIN.

KARS (cont) Why do you have a gun?

SENUR   It's my father's. He makes me carry it. For protection.

KEEPING THE GUN AIMED AT HER.

KARS   Your father?

SENUR   When I was … My mother was attacked. She was... He insists I carry it. For protection.

KARS   I see.

SENUR   (HOLDING OUT HER HAND) May I have it?

KARS (JOKING AROUND) And what's to stop me just shooting you now? What you said before – an injustice so obvious it beggars silence?

SENUR   It's not loaded.

KARS   Why carry it if it's not loaded?

SENUR   (CALMLY) A gun can scare people. It doesn't have to be loaded. They just have to think it is. May I have it?

KARS THINKS ABOUT IT, THEN TURNING IT HANDS IT BACK TO HER.

KARS   You shouldn't keep it there. It might fall out.

SENUR   (TAKING THE GUN) Thank you. Do you see any other place where I can put it? (SHE HOLDS IT, WEIGHING IT) Did I scare you?

KARS   My father is… He's a judge. He works in law enforcement.

SENUR   And?

KARS   I've seen a lot of guns.

SENUR   I see.

KARS   I wasn't scared.

KARS HAS JUST ABOUT FINISHED DRESSING

AND IS ABOUT TO CONTINUE WHEN THE MAIN DOORS OPEN AND THE JUDGE AND HIS WIFE APPEAR, LEADING THEIR GUESTS ONTO THE BALCONY, MUSIC BILLOWING OUT BEHIND THEM.

INSTINCTIVELY, WITHOUT THOUGHT, SENUR TURNS AND SHOOTS. THE FIRST SHOT CATCHES THE WIFE IN THE FACE AND SHE FALLS BACK, DEAD. NO ONE MOVES. SHE ADJUSTS AND SHOOTS THE JUDGE IN THE SHOULDER.

NOW THE CROWD SCREAMS.

LIGHTS DOWN.

END OF SCENE 1.

SCENE 2

CAR LIGHTS SHINE OUT ACROSS THE STAGE. A CAR COMES TO A HALT AND STOPS. CAR DOORS OPEN. TWO MEN – ONE LARGE, ONE SMALL – WALK OUT ONTO THE STAGE AND LOOK OUT AT A BUILDING OFF STAGE.

THOUGH BOTH ARE CARRYING GUNS THIS IS CLEARLY A DIFFERENT TIME, AND THEIR CLOTHES ARE OLD AND RUSTIC. THE TWO MEN ARE INDIGENOUS TO THE LAND. THEIR DRESS AND MANNERISMS BETRAY AN INCOM-

PATIBILITY TO THE OPULENCE OF THE PARTY.

THE TWO MEN LOOK OUT FROM BEHIND THE CAR LIGHTS. THE OLDER ONE NODS AND THE YOUNG ONE HANDS HIM HIS RIFLE BEFORE RETURNING TO THE CAR.

THE OLD MAN CALMLY RAISES HIS RIFLE IN THE AIR AND FIRES OFF A ROUND.

OLD   (CALLING OUT TO THE HOUSEHOLD OFF STAGE) Might as well come out! This doesn't have to be any worse than it is. Don't want us coming in to get you.

SILENCE.

THE YOUNG MAN RETURNS TO HIM, HOLDING TWO OLD-STYLE BURNING TORCHES, UNLIT, AND A CAN OF ACCELERANT.

THE OLD MAN IS LISTENING.

YOUNG   Want me to light them?

OLD   Not yet.

SILENCE. THE TWO MEN LISTEN.

YOUNG   What do you reckon's happening?

OLD   Looking out the back, no doubt. You see a movement back there...

THEY HEAR SOMETHING THAT WE CANNOT. THEY PAUSE AND LISTEN HARD.

YOUNG   What's he saying?

OLD   (SHOUTING OFF) You know what we're really here for! Might as well not make it any harder on yourselves!

SILENCE AS THEY LISTEN TO THE REPLY.

OLD (cont)   Yeah, well. He's not my god. Come on out now!

YOUNG   What's he talking about?

OLD   Smiting.

HE RAISES HIS GUN IN THE AIR AND FIRES AGAIN.

OLD (cont)   (SHOUTING OFF) No one gets hurt! You got my word on that. Come on out now and you'll be fair treated. Word given!

THEY LISTEN IN SILENCE.

YOUNG   Now?

OLD   Yeah, might as well.

THE YOUNGER MAN POURS ACCELERANT ON A TORCH AND, HOLDING IT OUT, LIGHTS IT. IT FLARES UP IN THE NIGHT LIGHT, ENGULFING THE TWO IN ITS SHADOWS.

HE IS ABOUT TO LIGHT THE SECOND BUT THE OLDER MAN PUTS HIS HAND ON HIS ARM.

OLD (cont)   (SHOUTING OFF) You see the way it is. Can't say you ain't had fair warning neither! Come on out now and no one will be harmed. Word of honour!

YOUNG   Can't barely make the back out with the light.

THEY LISTEN.

OLD   (SHOUTING OFF) This ain't something new to us! You understand me?

YOUNG   How you hear so good?

OLD   Listening.

THEY LISTEN.

YOUNG   What's he saying now?

OLD   (IGNORING HIM. SHOUTING OFF) I'm not here to debate with you. You got your reasons, same as me, but

THEY LISTEN.

YOUNG   What's they doing?

OLD   Reckon that's prayer. (HE HOLDS HIS HAND OUT FOR THE TORCH) Give that here.

THE YOUNGER MAN HANDS OVER THE TORCH. THE OLDER MAN POINTS HIS RIFLE TOWARDS THE BUILDING.

OLD (cont)   Run a line up, then. I've got you covered.

THE BOY STARTS TO POUR ACCELERANT IN THE DIRECTION OF THE HOMESTEAD AND SPLASHES IT TOWARDS THE BUILDING.

OLD (cont)   (SHOUTING OFF) Cold night and I ain't getting any younger! Dry enough though, I reckon. Dry enough for a dozen nights as I recall. Not sure the wood in there's gonna be any protection. Come on out now. No body's getting harmed. You got my word on that. Think of the children!

YOUNG   That'll do, you think?

OLD   (SHOUTING OFF) Think of the women! (TO THE YOUNGER MAN) You see movement out the back, you let me know. OK?

THEY LISTEN.

YOUNG   That's funny praying.

OLD   Wouldn't be praying if it didn't sound funny.

THEY LISTEN.

YOUNG   Gas won't last.

THE OLD MAN STEPS FORWARD AND FIRES ANOTHER SHOT INTO THE AIR.

OLD   (SHOUTING OFF) Listen now. All of you! This weren't your land! Weren't yours to build on. Not in law! Not in right! You know our customs. You know our ways. Plenty of places for prayer without you coming here, so stay or go, you've got our decision. One way or another. Stay or don't stay. I'm talking to all of you now. Young and old. You know your mind. You know our ways. You leave now and nothing's gonna happen to you, one way or another. Treated properly, and you have my word! You don't have to listen to any of them in there says different. Out front or out back, you have my word. But it's up to you!

FOR THE FIRST TIME, AS IF IN RESPONSE, WE HEAR THE SOUND OF PRAYER AND SINGING, JUST AUDIBLE AND DRIFTING ON THE WIND.

OLD   Light it.

THE YOUNG MAN DROPS THE TORCH ON THE GROUND. FLAMES LEAP UP TOWARDS THE BUILDING.

THOUGH THEY DIE OUT NEAR THE MEN IT IS CLEAR FROM THE LIGHT THAT THEY HAVE TAKEN HOLD OF THE BUILDING.

YOUNG   You reckon they'll leave?

OLD   Haven't met a man who doesn't fear fire over a swift run yet.

WE LISTEN TO THE SOUNDS OF PRAYER AND SINGING GROWING LOUDER.

YOUNG   Can't see nothing in these shadows.

THE OLD MAN TAKES THE RIFLE FROM THE YOUNGER, HIS NOW BEING EMPTY, AND STEPS FORWARD BEFORE FIRING REPEATEDLY INTO THE AIR.

OLD   (SHOUTING OFF) Fire! (LOUDER) Fire!!

THE SOUND OF SINGING HAS HALTED, REPLACED BY THE SOUND OF CRACKLING FIRE BUT THE SOUND OF PRAYER IS STILL STRONG. THE TWO MEN LISTEN.

YOUNG   You figure they heard?

THE FIRE IS HIGH NOW, THE LIGHT OF IT ILLUMINATING THE MEN MORE THAN THE CAR LIGHTS.

THE OLD MAN STUBS THE TORCH OUT CARE-FULLY ON THE GRASS.

THE SOUNDS OF PRAYER ON THE WIND BEGINS TO BE ACCOMPANIED BY SCREAMS, THOUGH WHETHER MALE OR FEMALE WE CANNOT MAKE OUT.

YOUNG   Think we should do something?

OLD   Like?

THE SOUNDS OF PRAYER HAVE CEASED, SCREAMS THE ONLY AUDIBLE SOUND.

SOMETHING INSIDE EXPLODES AND THE TWO MEN HAVE TO SHIELD THEMSELVES FROM THE HEAT OF THE BLAST.

THEY LISTEN.

THE SCREAMS HAVE STOPPED.

THE FIRELIGHT DIES.

THE OLD MAN SIGHS AND PREPARES TO GO.

YOUNG   Reckon they got out?

OLD   Damnedest thing I ever saw.

THEY HEAD BACK TO THE CAR.

YOUNG   What's done is done.

THE OLDER MAN PAUSES AND LOOKS AT THE YOUNGER.

OLD   No. No. Don't reckon it is. (HE MOVES TO EXIT) There'll be blood for this.

THEY EXIT TO THE CAR.

YOUNG   Long as it's not ours!

END OF SCENE 2.

SCENE 3

A SITTING ROOM IN THE JUDGE'S HOUSE, WARM AND DECADENT. THE FURNITURE IS OPULENT AND CLASSIC, THE WALLS BOOK-LINED AND ERUDITE. THIS IS CLEARLY NOT THE CENTRAL ROOM OF THE HOUSE BUT

NEVERTHELESS IS BOTH COMFORTABLE AND WELL USED.

UPSTAGE ARE THE DOORS THAT LEAD ONTO THE BALCONY THAT THE JUDGE ET AL HAD ENTERED FROM AT THE END OF SCENE 1.

ON ONE SIDE IS A DOOR LEADING TO THE REST OF THE HOUSE.

CENTRE A LARGE COUCH AND SURROUND-ING CHAIRS CIRCLE AN ORNATE RUG.

ON THE SOFA, UNDER A PROTECTIVE BLAN-KET, THE JUDGE, STRIPPED TO A SINGLET, IS BEING TREATED BY THE FAMILY PHYSICIAN WHO IS CLEARLY DRESSED FOR THE PARTY.

THE JUDGE, THOUGH OBVIOUSLY IN DISCOM-FORT AND PAIN, IS IN FULL COMMAND OF HIS FACULTIES AND IS CONSCIOUS WHILE THE DOCTOR REMOVES A BULLET FROM HIS SHOULDER.

A BOTTLE OF THE DAY IS CLAMPED IN THE JUDGE'S HANDS AS HE YELLS AT THE DOCTOR'S PROBING.

DOCTOR   Hold still, damn you!

JUDGE   God in heaven! It feels like you're taking a bone, not a bullet!

DOCTOR   It's surprisingly deep... There. Got it.

HE DROPS THE BULLET INTO A NEARBY GLASS.

DOCTOR (cont)   That makes three then, I suppose.

JUDGE   Four. The Wayan child.

DOCTOR   It's lucky it was a small calibre. The

closeness of it. Anyone would think bullets weren't for killing.

JUDGE   Sarah?

THE DOCTOR, PATCHING UP THE MAN'S SHOULDER, GIVES HIM A LOOK AND SHAKES HIS HEAD. THE JUDGE DRINKS IN SILENCE.

DOCTOR   We should leave it to the police.

JUDGE   The police! Most of them were right here at the party!

DOCTOR   The real police.

JUDGE   Did she...

DOCTOR   No. No, it would have been.... She wouldn't have felt a thing.

JUDGE   You done?

DOCTOR   For now. We need to get you to a hospital. You can keep it like that for now, but you're going to need stitches and infection...

JUDGE   Not the first time I've been shot.

DOCTOR   This isn't then. We're not young men anymore.

JUDGE   Hospitals complicate things. Police complicate things. We need to know what she knows. Where's Diarmen?

DOCTOR   He's got her downstairs.

JUDGE   Well, bring her up here!

DOCTOR   For the last time...

JUDGE   Just do it, will you? Be my friend for a minute, not my physician.

THE DOCTOR THINKS AND THEN MOVES TO LEAVE.

DOCTOR   Five minutes, then we get you to a hospital, alright?

JUDGE   Get the boy in here, too.

THE DOCTOR GOES OVER TO THE DOOR AND LOOKS OUT AS IF TO SHOUT. HE SEES SOMEONE OFF-STAGE AND NODS. THEY'VE HEARD EVERYTHING AND DON'T NEED TELLING.

MEANWHILE THE JUDGE DRINKS HEAVILY FROM A BOTTLE, AND REACHES PAINFULLY FOR A FRAMED PICTURE ON THE COFFEE TABLE OF HIS WIFE. HE LOOKS AT IT LOVINGLY, BUT AS SOON AS HE SEES THE DOCTOR RETURNING HE STUFFS IT BEHIND HIM DOWN THE BACK OF THE SOFA AND RETURNS TO THE BOTTLE.

DOCTOR   They're coming.

THE TWO MEN WAIT. THE DOCTOR PACES.

JUDGE   How'd you forget the Wayan boy anyway?

DOCTOR   I just did.

JUDGE   He was aiming at you!

DOCTOR   Aiming isn't shooting. (RECOGNIZING THE ERROR) Sorry.

DIARMEN ENTERS, SENUR SLUMPED UNCONSCIOUS OVER HIS SHOULDER. THERE IS BLOOD AROUND HER EAR.

A BIG MAN, DIARMEN IS OLDER BUT STILL

VITAL, AND THOUGH HIS CLOTHES ARE EX-
PENSIVE AND HIS MOVEMENTS REFINED HE
IS CLEARLY NOT UNACCUSTOMED TO VIO-
LENCE.

KARS ENTERS BEHIND HIM.

JUDGE   Put her in the chair.

DIARMEN DEPOSITS HER ROUGHLY IN A
DINING CHAIR AND TIES HER ARMS TO THE
CHAIR.

KARS   What are we doing?

JUDGE   (TO DOCTOR) Did you check her?

DOCTOR   A concussion, nothing more.

KARS What are we doing?

JUDGE   (TO DIARMEN) Weapons? (DIAR-
MEN NODS) Properly this time?

DIARMEN   She's clean.

JUDGE   Tie her. The string's in the... (HE
POINTS PAINFULLY) In there.

KARS Pa?

JUDGE   (TO KARS) Get me another bottle of
whisky, would you?

KARS   Sir...

JUDGE   I'm fine, I'll... I'm going to the hospital
directly...

KARS   Mother...

JUDGE   I know. I'm sorry.

KARS   She just shot her.

JUDGE   Me too!

KARS   Shouldn't we go to the police?

JUDGE   This... She killed your mother, Kars! God's sake boy, she walked into our home, ate our food, drank our wine, shot your mother, and tried to kill me! What do you want me to do?! Hand her over to the authorities? Lock her up? Get her some counselling for fuck's sake? She killed your mother!

KARS   Stepmother.

JUDGE   What was that?

KARS   She killed my stepmother!

JUDGE   It's time for you to grow a pair of balls, my boy. Not just a cock!

KARS   She was talking about the murder. Before. At the party.

JUDGE   Get me a bottle of whiskey, would you. The good stuff. I need a level head for this and my shoulder's killing me!

EXIT KARS

DOCTOR   Karl...

JUDGE   It was for the... It was for the boy! Damn it, Hankle! Do you think..? It was for the boy!

DIARMEN She's awake.

JUDGE   Yes, I know. (TO SENUR) We don't have much time. Do you hear me? Why did you do this? Come on! I know you can hear me!

DIARMEN MOVES FORWARD. SENUR OPENS HER EYES AND LOOKS AT THE JUDGE.

SENUR   I wanted to kill you!

JUDGE   Yes, well. Good luck with that. You killed an innocent woman!

SENUR   There are no innocents.

DIARMEN MOVES FORWARD QUICKLY AND STRIKES HER. THE JUDGE ADJUSTS HIS WOUNDED SHOULDER.

JUDGE   Alright, alright!

DOCTOR   I gave birth to that woman! With these hands! Innocent? There was no creature more innocent...

JUDGE   (LOOKING AT DIARMEN) Yes, well, I wouldn't go that far.

ENTER KARS

JUDGE   You came into my home and tried to kill me. Kill my wife! (SENUR LOOKS AWAY) Alright, you came into my house and tried to kill me. Why? Why did you wait so late? Why not simply kill me when you walked in.

SENUR LOOKS AT KARS

SENUR   I wanted you to suffer.

KARS MOVES FORWARD TO STRIKE HER BUT IS BLOCKED BY DIARMEN

KARS   You fucking bitch!

JUDGE   Alright! Alright! Would you three please... God! Give me the whisky!

DIARMEN UNCORKS AND PASSES THE JUDGE THE NEW BOTTLE. HE TAKES A SWIG.

DOCTOR   This has gone on...

THE JUDGE WAVES HIM OFF.

JUDGE   That's better. Now... What do you know about the murder of Khadife Sedat?

SENUR   Nothing.

KARS   You lying whore!

DOCTOR   You were talking about her. Everyone heard!

JUDGE   Was she a friend of yours? Come on, you might as well tell us!

SENUR   I know nothing about her.

DIARMEN Do you want me to...

JUDGE   In a few moments, my good friend here is going to insist I hand you over to the authorities. Even if he doesn't there were enough people who saw what you did. Word is bound to reach them, no matter how well absorbed my guests are. At least one of them is going to have the foresight to call a newspaper, who in turn are going to call the authorities... So you see, no matter what crimes you've committed here, I can assure you if you know anything about the murder of Khadife Sedat then we are your best bet on surviving the night.

SENUR   I know she was murdered. I know that you were the judge in the case.

JUDGE   I am the judge in every case.

SENUR   I know you let her murderer go!

KARS   You know nothing!

JUDGE   Do you...

A PHONE RINGS BOTH IN THE ROOM AND ELSEWHERE.

DOCTOR   Your time is up child.

JUDGE   (TO DIARMEN) Take it downstairs.

EXIT DIARMEN.

ALL LISTEN AS HE LEAVES THE ROOM. THE PHONE CONTINUES RINGING. THEY WAIT. THE PHONE STOPS, HAVING BEEN PICKED UP.

KARS   I think we should...

JUDGE   Do you know who I am?

SENUR   Yes.

JUDGE   I am the high judge official. That means I oversee cases. I oversaw the case of Khadife Sedat. And yes, you're right. I threw the case out. Do you know why?

KARS   What has this got to do with...

SENUR   You got your fat friend off.

JUDGE   The senator? No. No, I threw the case out because there was no proof. Oh, there was, trust me, mountains of it, to begin with. Fingerprints, eye witnesses... But all of these have a habit of going away. Little by little. One by one. Senator Matgolise is a very... powerful man. Very powerful and... Well. The authorities are very corrupt. Something I thought we had taken care of but... That is the law! We make laws and we must follow them. No matter how badly people treat them.

SANUR   Are you going to torture me?

JUDGE   Probably. Does that frighten you? Like

I said, there are laws. Men's laws. And there are God's laws as well, but you know which ones are most important? Men's! God's laws, well, they're perfect and perfection doesn't need help from anyone. But men's laws… I spent… Have you ever read our constitution? I spent months on it. Months! The best minds, the best men, and still it's imperfect! You see, God's laws, they are in the heart. Men's laws are made of words and words can be corrupted, so we must help them. We must help them with the truth! That's how you help words. You shine the light of truth on them and find the bits where it seeps through!

KARS   Stop it!

JUDGE   Other men have no such qualms. They don't want to shine the light of truth on things. They use words like shields. Like things to hide behind! Even words we make!

KARS   Enough.

JUDGE   My son has a kind heart but we both know, don't we? We both know that men who hide behind words will do anything to keep those words protecting them! They have the police and they have the judiciary and they will kill you. If I let them. So, you see, no matter what we think of you… No matter what you've done here…. No matter what, we….

KARS   Everyone out!

DOCTOR   Kars…

KARS   Out! Now! I want to talk to my father!

DOCTOR   Thus is not the time…

DIARMEN RE-ENTERS. THE THREE MEN LOOK AT HIM.

DIARMEN SHAKES HIS HEAD.

DIARMEN Caterers.

KARS   I mean it! OUT! Now! I need to talk to my father!

THE JUDGE LOOKS TIRED BUT HE NODS TO THE TWO MEN WHO MOVE TO GO.

DIARMEN   The girl?

KARS   I want her to hear this!

DOCTOR   I'll see to the body.

EXIT DOCTOR.

DIARMEN   You sure?

JUDGE   He calls no one!

DIARMEN NODS AND EXITS.

JUDGE   Pass me a glass, would you?

KARS THINKS ABOUT IT.

JUDGE (cont)   Pass me a glass!

THE BOY ACQUIESCES AND GOES TO GET A GLASS.

JUDGE   (TO SENUR) I spoil him, I know. But blood will do that. Also, his mother just died.

SENUR   Stepmother.

THE JUDGE GLARES AT HER IN ANGER, THEN TAKES THE GLASS FROM KARS AND HOLDS IT OUT FOR HIM TO POUR, WHICH THE BOY DOES.

JUDGE   Say it then.

BUT KARS IS TOO ANGRY TO SPEAK. HIS HAND SHAKES AS HE POURS THE DRINK.

JUDGE (cont) Don't worry about her. She'll be dead before daybreak.

KARS   How can you…? How can you! It's... She's not even dead an hour and...

JUDGE   Don't you dare! You didn't even... (HE YIELDS, SIPS HIS DRINK.) That was harsh. Shock, I suppose. The mechanism.

KARS   I know you! I know that tone!

JUDGE   Kars…

KARS   Kill her! Kill her and be done with it. Diarmen...

THE JUDGE IS SHOCKED BY THIS.

KARS (cont.) It's what you want. Don't deny it! (TO SENUR) You're going to die, bitch! You think...

JUDGE   Stop it! Stop it. You know that's not...

KARS   This woman...!

JUDGE   She's a girl!

KARS   Diarmen...

JUDGE   That is not what we do!

SENUR   It's what I do! If you don't have the…!

JUDGE   Shut your mouth or I'll have it shut for you!

SILENCE

JUDGE   Kars... Listen...

KARS   What have you got her here for if not...

JUDGE   Listen....

KARS   No, I won't. I won't listen to any more

of... (HE POINTS TO THE BOTTLE) This!

JUDGE   (LOUDLY) You will. You will! You will listen! She was my wife – mine! Stepmother? She was my wife! But... There are bigger questions here! Bigger...

KARS   I don't...

JUDGE   Matgolise is... There are holes, do you understand this? Real holes! Corruption! And... I don't know how high up it goes. I don't know how far it goes! Why do you... The reason for this party tonight was to work out where our weaknesses....

KARS THROWS THE BOTTLE ACROSS THE ROOM AND IT SMASHES ON THE WALL.

THE JUDGE RISES SHARPLY TO CONFRONT HIM.

JUDGE   We are weak! Understand me? You think someone could have come in here and tried to assassinate me... We are weak! And we are paying for it! I am trying to maint... I will have justice! In this country! And I am...

THE DOOR OPENS AND DIARMEN ENTERS, ALERTED BY THE NOISE.

DIARMEN   Is everything alright?

JUDGE SLUMPS INTO THE CHAIR AGAIN.

JUDGE   We decided to take a vow of abstinence.

KARS STORMS PAST THEM.

KARS   Do what you want but I'm telling you this! If you don't put a bullet in her head, I will!

EXIT KARS.

JUDGE   (TO SENUR) Don't mind my son. Blood will be spoilt.

SENUR   He is a playboy.

DIARMEN   What's that about?

JUDGE   The Doctor?

DIARMEN With...

HE GESTURES. THE JUDGE NODS.

JUDGE   Good. Quickly then. Help me! Shut the door and... Try to keep your dick in your pants this time. (TO SENUR) What's your name?

SENUR   My name is Senur Kafii.

JUDGE   Do you know what is happening here?

SENUR   You want to hurt me. But you won't.

JUDGE   Don't tempt me! Did you know Khad-ife Sedat?

SENUR   I know you let her murderer go free.

JUDGE   But you didn't know her?

SENUR   No, I did not.

JUDGE   There's no point lying to us!

SENUR   (BEAT) I wish I had. I wish I were able to avenge her as well, but... I only know what I read in the papers. What people say in bars.

DIARMEN   She could be lying.

JUDGE   No, no. I don't think she is. So. Why are you here? Why kill me?

SENUR   There are thousands who want you

dead!

JUDGE   (TO DIARMEN) Who did she come with?

DIARMEN   I don't know.

JUDGE   Her accent, her clothes... The two don't match. Did everyone sign the guest book?

DIARMEN.   I think so.

JUDGE   Check the book! I want to know who she came with.

DIARMEN   She could have used a false name.

JUDGE   Did you?

SENUR SHAKES HER HEAD.

JUDGE (cont)   Check the book.

DIARMEN   I don't suppose you'd save us the effort? (TO JUDGE) I can get it out of her.

THE TWO MEN LOOK AT HER.

JUDGE   Check the book first. And disconnect the phones. If you haven't already.

DIARMEN   First thing I thought of.

THE JUDGE NODS AND DIARMEN EXITS.

JUDGE   We were never friends, you know. Matgolise and I. Conspirators, maybe, but never friends.

SENUR   The corrupt die!

JUDGE   Not in my experience! (PAUSE) You are not the first assassin they have sent to kill me.

SENUR   Just the last!

JUDGE   Shall I tell you a story?

SENUR   Let me tell you one.

JUDGE   Is it short?

SENUR   We came to this land two hundred years ago. Three generations!

JUDGE   I think you don't understand what we mean by short.

SENUR   We came to this land two hundred years ago. Was it ours? Was it ours to take?

JUDGE   Is this irony? I hate irony!

SENUR   We came to this land two hundred years ago, and when we came to this land we owned it. We owned it. It was ours. There were no cities. There was no progression. When a swallow takes a tree for its nest...

JUDGE   Why a swallow?

SENUR   Does it care what other birds have lived in the branches? Does it look for... Remnants of nests... Twigs that indicate that a decade ago a robin blessed its branches?

JUDGE   That's a bit simplistic.

SENUR   Yesterday, then? Does it care about yesterday? Does the tree care about the woodlice that infested its bark? No. It roots them out, kills them!

JUDGE   Supremacist nonsense!

SENUR   But we come, we take the land. Own the land. Write writs of ownership. And then teach them to read these! (PAUSE) One per cent of the population...

JUDGE   We don't have time...

SENUR   Root them out! Kill them! Burn everything they have and erase them from the face of the earth. That's the way we used to do it. That's the way we were made! Inside!

JUDGE   You don't strike me as a nationalist.

SENUR   We steal their property and then we teach them what property means!

JUDGE   Let me tell you my story! There was... He was a boy. Really. No more than eight or ten and he... As part of my mandate I overseer cases... I follow up on judicial inquiries. Bad justice! So I have this boy. No more than eight or ten. Couldn't have been more than seven or eight when he killed them, and he stands in front of me. A young man! A young man, guilty of the most terrible crimes, but he stands in front of me not because of what he's done but because of who he is. And who he is, is a refugee. Not black, not poor, but a refugee nonetheless. And the question before me was, did he get convicted based on what he did or based on who he was and... I had to judge. I had to look that boy in the eye and judge... Judge him! His very soul, you understand?

SENUR   What had he done?

JUDGE   He had killed his pregnant sister. I don't think he knew she was pregnant. I don't think he knew what it meant. He might even have been trying to help her... We'll never know. But I had to look into his eyes and judge... Judge his soul.... Much as I'm doing now. That was this morning.

SENUR   And? Had he?

JUDGE   He was an evil little bastard that de-
served everything he got and I locked him up till he
gets it. Khadife Sedat was not that. There are men of
power, Senur. Men who can change your life. And
we all understand that. We do, but there are bigger,
bigger things than that! Bigger... If someone put you
up to this...?

SENUR   No one put me up to this.

JUDGE   If someone did...

SENUR   Is that how I strike you? As an assassin? A hired gun?

JUDGE   Honestly?

SENUR   Girl with a gun? Femme fatale?

JUDGE   You are. A girl with a gun.

SENUR   Do you have a picture of her? Something you keep in your wallet, perhaps. I hear people
do that. Keep pictures of loved ones in their pocket.
Is that what she was to you? A loved one? Or was she
some trophy? Something to hang on your arm.

JUDGE   Men don't do that.

SENUR   Was she beautiful? I never really got a
good look.

SILENCE.

THE JUDGE REACHES BEHIND HIM PAINFULLY
AND PULLS OUT THE PHOTO FRAME.

JUDGE   Every day. Every day. You won't pro-
voke me, you see. Men try it every day.

SENUR   Do they all shoot your wife?

THE JUDGE STARTS TO REMOVE THE PHOTO

FROM THE FRAME, WANTING TO TOUCH IT, TOUCH HER.

JUDGE   She was beautiful. Not in the way you mean, but she was beautiful. Ilsa... I was married before. Ilsa was.... on the outside. Very young. Very beautiful. It's hard being married to a woman like that. A beautiful woman. Someone you... When I... The second time...

SENUR   How did she die? Your first wife?

JUDGE   Does it matter?

SENUR   For you? (THE JUDGE NODS) Twice then women have died because of you.

THE JUDGE IS ANGERED.

SENUR (cont) Hit me! Go on. I want you to hit me. Your son has more balls than you! I want you to hit me! Show me your true side!

JUDGE   Like yours?

SENUR   Look at her. Look at her! Yesterday she was warmth in your bed, today she is cold on the floor! Look at her!

THE JUDGE IS CRYING. HE STROKES THE FACE IN THE PHOTO AND TRIES TO CONTAIN HIM-SELF.

JUDGE   I don't... Never...

SENUR   Yesterday she was fucking your friend and now she's...

JUDGE   We... It's complicated. You don't know that.

SENUR   Everyone   knows   that!   The   world

knows that. They laugh at you! Behind your back. The judge's wife! His comrade-in-arms, fucking his wife!

JUDGE   You don't know what you're talking about.

SENUR   Does it only work as a pendulum these days?

JUDGE   She was... Lonely... I…

SENUR   Aren't you glad I shot her face off?

THE JUDGE ERUPTS. HE RISES QUICKLY AND YANKS HER HAIR BACK. SHE LOOKS PLEASED.

JUDGE   You don't talk about her! You don't talk about her!

SENUR   Dead. Whore!

WITH A SCREAM THE JUDGE SCREWS UP THE PHOTO AND STUFFS IT INTO HER MOUTH. HE IS SCREAMING WORDLESS PAIN AT HER, HIS FACE AN INCH FROM HER OWN. SHE WATCHES HIM, HALF FIGHTING, HALF ENJOYING HIS TORMENT.

SHOCKED AT HIMSELF HE STEPS BACK BREATHLESS, SILENT, MOUTH OPEN. SHE WATCHES HIM CALMLY, CHEWING THE PHOTO INTO A SODDEN PULP. THEN SHE SMILES AND SPITS IT INTO HIS FACE.

HE IS SHOCKED, AS MUCH AT HIMSELF AS HER AND STEPS FORWARD, ALMOST TENDERLY, REACHING FOR HER WITH HIS GOOD HAND.

AS HE DRAWS CLOSE SHE SPRINGS, PUSHING UP WITH HER FEET, THROWING HERSELF AT

HIM. SHE HITS HIM FULL FORCE AND THEY BOTH FALL BACK, WITH HER ON TOP OF HIM. HE SCREAMS IN PAIN.

SHE BITES DEEP INTO HIS SHOULDER AND THIS TIME THE SCREAM IS INTENSE. HE IS TRYING TO PULL HER OFF BUT SHE TEARS AT HIS WOUNDED SHOULDER IN ANIMALISTIC FURY.

THE DOOR OPENS, AND THE DOCTOR AND DIARMEN RUSH IN. THE DOCTOR IS TAKEN ABACK BUT DIARMEN DOESN'T HESITATE. HE LIFTS ANOTHER CHAIR AND BRING IT DOWN ON HER HEAD.

SHE FALLS UNCONSCIOUS AS WE SMASH TO BLACKOUT.

END OF ACT 1.

ACT 2

SCENE 1

A HOUSE, POOR AND RUSTIC. THOUGH UN-KNOWN TO THE AUDIENCE THIS IS THE HOME OF YOUNG FROM ACT 1.

IF THERE IS ANY DECORATION, IT IS SPARSE. IF ANY FURNITURE IT IS OLDER THAN THE COU-PLE WHO LIVE THERE.

THERE HAS BEEN A FIGHT.

ANISI LIES CENTRE STAGE, HER POOR DRESS TORN, HER STATE DISHEVELLED, HER FACE TO THE AUDIENCE. SHE HAS JUST BEEN RAPED.

BEHIND HER KIFUR IS CROUCHED, A BLOOD-IED BOTTLE IN HIS HAND.

THOUGH BETTER DRESSED THAN ANISI, KIFUR IS STILL NOT WEALTHY. HIS CLOTHES SHOWS SIGNS OF WEAR AND ARE DISHEVELLED FROM THE EFFORT OF THE RAPE.

HE LOOKS LOST IN A TRANCE. ANISI, STILL RESOLUTE, MAKES NO MOVEMENT TO PUSH AWAY.

SLOWLY KIFUR SEES THE BOTTLE IN HIS HAND, REGISTERS THE BLOOD ON IT, AND TOSSES IT AWAY IN DISGUST. HE STARTS TO WIPE HIS HAND ON HIS CLOTHES AND THINKS TWICE ABOUT IT. HE SCUTTLES AWAY AND LOOKS AT THE WOMAN WHO STILL DOESN'T MOVE.

KIFUR   Do you understand. (SILENCE) I need to know if you understand.

ANISI   Yes.

KIFUR   Yes, I understand or...

ANISI   (SOTTO) I understand.

KIFUR   I didn't...

ANISI   I understand. (SILENCE) May I move now?

KIFUR   I need you to under... Yes, you can move. I.. Of course.

SHE GATHERS HER SKIRT AROUND HER BUT DOES NOT RISE.

KIFUR (cont)   This is not my way. It's not... I need you to understand. I need... I took no pleasure in it.

SILENCE.

KIFUR (cont)   This is your way. His way. My sister was.... When she was young... When we were children... My sister was. She was... Colourful. Boyish. Our father... He was not a simple man. Kind but... So there was punishment. For... Misbehaviour. Punishment. And my sister was colourful so... Punishment. It was her that decided to come here. Her faith. My father... It is not our way, you understand this? Not our... She burnt. Alive, they tell me. Burnt alive... And... It's not our way. To leave the house. Like that. In... It is not our way. A woman should be covered. We believe this and... It was her faith. You understand this? Her way. Your husband... He should be here. To answer for his crimes. He should be here. So this is your law. Your way. A wife... Taking the punishment for her husband's crimes. I am trying to....

SILENCE.

KIFUR (cont)   You must be cold.

SILENCE. SHE SHIFTS SLIGHTLY.

ANISI   He will kill you.

KIFUR   Your husband?

ANISI   He will kill you.

KIFUR   I am following his law.

SILENCE.

KIFUR (cont)   You told me your name. I don't remember it. I should know your name. Was it... Anisi?

ANISI   He will come and he will kill you.

KIFUR   He killed my sister. Burnt her alive.

ANISI   He will kill you.

KIFUR   This isn't... This is the law! Not my
law! This is how you judge yourselves. I didn't... For-
eigners invade your lands? Burn them! A husband
breaks the law, his wife... I didn't want to do this! I
didn't want to... This is your law! He killed... My sister... He should have been here! For justice! I didn't
want to do this!

SILENCE. SHE IS SHIVERING, PERHAPS FROM
THE COLD, PERHAPS FROM BLOOD LOSS, BUT
STILL SHE IS RESOLUTE.

KIFUR (cont) It is, it's cold in here. I don't know if
there are... You shouldn't be cold.

SILENCE.

HE MOVES CLOSER TO HER. SHE PREVENTS HERSELF FROM FLINCHING. PREVENTS HIM FROM SEEING HER FLINCH.

KIFUR (cont)   Are you cold? I don't... I don't want to...

SOUNDLESSLY HE MOVES IN AND EMBRACES HER, WARMING HER.

IT IS NOT SEXUAL, BUT IT IS COMPASSION-ATE. HE IS CAREFUL NOT TO GET HIS BLOOD STAINED HAND ON HER CLOTHES.

NOW HER FACADE CRACKS, HER RESOLUTION GONE, STRIPPED AWAY BY THE INTIMACY, THE TENDERNESS OF THE MOMENT. HER STOICISM IS STRIPPED AWAY AND UNSEEN BY KIFUR SHE SCREAMS SILENTLY IN TERROR.

OFF-STAGE WE HEAR THE MIRRORED SOUND OF SENUR, SCREAMING IN PAIN.

END OF SCENE 1 .

SCENE 2

WE ARE BACK IN THE ROOM AT THE JUDGES HOUSE. SENUR IS STILL TIED TO THE CHAIR AND DIARMEN HAS JUST RIPPED HER FINGER-NAIL OUT. SHE IS SCREAMING IN AGONY.

ON THE OTHER SIDE OF THE ROOM KARS WATCHES UNCOMFORTABLY, CLEARLY DIS-

TURBED BY WHAT HE IS SEEING.

KARS   Shit!

SENUR LAUGHS AND SPITS IN DIARMEN'S FACE. HE SLAPS HER BACKHANDEDLY, AND THE CHAIR TOPPLES OVER.

KARS (cont)   Shit!

DIARMEN MOVES TO PICK HER UP.

DIARMEN   She tried to kill your father. Twice! She already killed your stepmother. Would you have me read poetry?

SENUR   Is that it?

KARS (ANGERED INTO ACTION) Why are you here? Who sent you!?

SENUR   (TO KARS) Little boy with a little cock!

DIARMEN LEANS IN AND SQUEEZES THE FINGERNAIL HE JUST PULLED OFF. SHE SCREAMS.

KARS   You came with Taimor. What does he have to do with this? What does he have to do with you?

SENUR   I work with him.

DIARMEN   How?

SENUR   How?

KARS   What are you doing to us?

SENUR   What does it look like? I'm destroying you! His lover. Your father! His career! All of it. I'm destroying your whole family. (BEAT) Tell me, has it started to itch yet?

KARS IS TAKEN ABACK. DIARMEN ROUNDS ON

HER.

DIARMEN   Suddenly you're talkative, is that it? Good! Then talk to me. You understand? (SILENCE) You came with Taimor. He is working with Matgolise. I have a couple of questions for you. There are nine more fingers. Ten more toes. Questions and answers. Alright? I am not the judge. Understand?

SENUR   I understand.

HE CLAMPS THE PLIERS ONTO ANOTHER FINGERNAIL.

DIARMEN   Good. What is the connection between Matgolise and Taimor?

SENUR   Nothing.

HE YANKS OUT ANOTHER FINGERNAIL. IT'S HARD. EXCRUCIATING. SHE SCREAMS.

KARS   Whore! Fucking… whore!

DIARMEN   (TO SENUR) Hey! Hey, do not pass out on me! Come on! Do you understand me? Do not pass out!

KARS   Fuck!

SENUR   Yes.

DIARMEN   Yes?

SENUR   Yes, there is a connection.

DIARMEN   Between Matgolise and Taimor? Answer me! What connection. Hey! Hey! What connection?

SENUR   (MOTIONING TO KARS) Ask him.

DIARMEN   What? What does that mean?

KARS   The... you lying whore!

SENUR   Ask him who his lover is!

DIARMEN   Enough. The senator is in on this. He will be brought to justice! They will all be. However many of them! Now, tell me what I need to know!

SENUR   (TO KARS) Have you pissed yet? Tell me.

DIARMEN   How many people in the Senate? How many of them knew about the attack! Tell me and I will spare your life. Tell me and I promise you! A day in court. I promise you!

KARS SCRATCHES HIMSELF.

SENUR   There! It itches! Tied to a chair I am beating you!

DIARMEN   What is she talking about?

SENUR   Little boy, little cock!

KARS IS WHITE NOW.

DIARMEN   Kars? What is she talking about?

SENUR   (TO DIARMEN) Tell me, are there any cuts on your hands?

DIARMEN LOOKS AT HER BLOOD ON HIS HANDS AND WIPES THEM QUICKLY. HE ROUNDS ON KARS.

DIARMEN   What did you do?

KARS   It wasn't like that.

DIARMEN LOOKS AT SENUR, THEN AT KARS. HE BEGINS TO WIPE HIS HANDS OBSESSIVELY.

DIARMEN   You stupid little boy!

KARS   It wasn't like that.

DIARMEN   Wasn't it? Yes, I'm sure you put up an extensive fight!

KARS   Oh God!

SENUR   Tied to a chair!

DIARMEN   Quickly now. How do you know her?

KARS   I don't. I.... She... We met here. At the party!

DIARMEN   Just like that?

KARS   She was on the balcony and...

DIARMEN   And you didn't know her before?

KARS   No, never!

DIARMEN   I mean you'd never met her before?

KARS   No. I swear it.

PAUSE.

DIARMEN   Just like that. You fuck her. Just like that?

KARS   On the balcony. She...

DIARMEN   Alright. Alright! God.

SENUR   Little boys playing.

DIARMEN   Well, if you didn't know her... We... Look, we'll get you tested but...

SENUR LAUGHS.

KARS   Little bitch!

DIARMEN   Kars. KARS! It's.. She's probably... You're fine! You hear me. There's no reason to think she's got...

SENUR   But I do! All of it! I made sure of it! I...

KARS   (DESPAIRING) Argh!

DIARMEN   Listen to me. Listen! I need you to... You've got blood on you. See. Blood!

KARS   It's mother's.

DIARMEN   Well, let's be sure of it, shall we. Go wash it off.

KARS   God... What if I...

DIARMEN   Wash it off. Take a shower. Have you taken one since you... No, alright. Go take a shower. Yes? Leave this one to me, alright? Kars! Take a shower!

KARS   Right. Yes. Yes, you're right.

DIARMEN   Go. Quickly now.

KARS   You're... Right.

DIARMEN   Change your clothes.

EXIT KARS.

SENUR   Run little boy!

DIARMEN TURNS AND PULLS A CHAIR UP IN FRONT OF SENUR BEFORE SITTING.

DIARMEN   Just you and me now. No parlour tricks. Just little bits of truth, alright?

SENUR   You won't be pulling any more nails though, will you!

DIARMEN   You really think I have to touch you? Is that what you think? (PAUSE) During the war there was this man. A general. And… He didn't want to face what he had done. To the people. So, I tracked him to this cave. High… Long time. I followed and followed. Really high! Right on the border. And he hid. In this cave. He had food and he had water, and I suppose he thought I wouldn't see him there. Wouldn't track him. Pass him by. So, he hid. (PAUSE) I had six shots. Seven at best. You wouldn't think it but bullets are very hard to come by in a war. That's all I had. Seven at best. And I told him. I called into the cave and I told him. Told him exactly what I am telling you here now. That I am a patient man! And… Every time he came out, I put a bullet in him. Not a death shot. Not to kill him. A nick. Just to drive him back into the cave. Seven bullets. Maximum. And him with all that food! But I didn't want to shoot him. I wanted him to suffer. The way we suffered. Seven bullets. And still he starved to death!

SENUR   You were there, weren't you? That day. I'd forgotten it until now. I could only remember his face but it was you, wasn't it?

DIARMEN   What do you do for Taimor?

SENUR   I don't do anything for him. I fetch papers, answer the telephone…

DIARMEN What do you mean?

SENUR   I work at his office. Assisting.

DIARMEN   I don't believe you.

SILENCE.

DIARMEN (cont)   Why would a senator bring an assistant to one of these things?

SENUR   To impress her. To impress her because

she is young and he thinks she is pretty and...

DIARMEN   I don't believe you.

SENUR   It happens all the time.

DIARMEN What happened with the boy?

SENUR   I killed him.

DIARMEN   Why hasn't he called? The senator? Taimor. Why hasn't he called? We all saw you. We all saw you... He would have called. If this was all innocent. He would have called!

SENUR   She had a pretty face. Did you like to kiss her face? Before I blew it off.

DIARMEN   Why hasn't he called?

SENUR   Did you flinch from it? When you saw it? After. That face you kissed. Would you kiss it now?

DIARMEN   How many people? Who is coming for us? Why? Is the hospital safe?

HE RISES AND GOES TO THE PHONE.

DIARMEN (cont) If I call him now. If I make a call. Will he tell me? Pretty girl he's trying to impress. Will he say that?

SENUR   You unplugged the phone.

DIARMEN   I am a very patient man.

SENUR   Why do you work for him? Still. After all these years, why do you still work for him?

DIARMEN   I can wait forever!

SENUR   It was her, wasn't it? You loved her. She loved you. (NODDING TO THE DOOR) Is he even his?

CALMLY AND WITHOUT FUSS HE UNHOL-
STERS HIS GUN AND PLAYS WITH IT.

DIARMEN   How many? Who? Why?

SENUR   All those years and you still stayed
with him!

HE RISES AND CALMLY POINTS THE GUN IN
HER FACE.

DIARMEN   I won't repeat it.

SENUR   You looked just like that. Just like that!
I thought it was him but...

DIARMEN   Last...

A POWERFUL SHOT RINGS OUT. AN OBJECT
NEAR SENUR'S HEAD EXPLODES. BOTH DIAR-
MEN AND SENUR FLINCH.

KARS ENTERS, A SHOTGUN IN HIS HANDS. IT IS
LARGE AND UNWIELDY AND HE IS WALKING
TOWARDS THEM, STILL DRESSED IN THE SAME
CLOTHES AS BEFORE BUT WITHOUT HIS JACK-
ET.

HE IS BARELY ON THE STAGE WHEN DIAR-
MEN, ACTING COMPLETELY ON INSTINCT AT
THE SOUND OF THE GUNSHOT, TURNS AND
SHOOTS HIM IN THE CHEST.

THE BOY LOOKS SURPRISED AND SHOOTS
WILDLY INTO THE CEILING BEFORE FALLING
DOWN.

DIARMEN   Kars!

HE RUSHES OVER TO THE BOY AND PRESSES

AGAINST THE WOUND.

DIARMEN (cont) Kars!

KARS TRIES TO SPEAK BUT HE CAN'T BREATHE. HIS ARMS FLAP AT HIS SIDES.

DIARMEN (cont) Kars! Stay with... KARS! We'll...

BUT THE BOY IS DEAD.

SENUR IS RECOVERING FROM THE SHOTGUN BLAST NEXT TO HER HEAD.

DIARMEN (cont) Kars.

SENUR   Blood for blood.

DIARMEN Shut up.

SENUR   I killed a woman today!

HE TURNS AND POINTS THE GUN AT HER.

SENUR (cont) I was aiming for a man, but I guess no one is a good shot in this house.

HE LOWERS THE GUN ONCE MORE AND TURNS TO KARS.

SENUR (cont) Just a boy, wasn't he. Just a stupid, young... I killed a woman today. I didn't mean to. I was aiming for the man. Perhaps I should have been aiming at you. You loved her. His woman. Did you love him too?

DIARMEN   No.

SENUR   I meant her husband. Did you love him? (PAUSE) When I was young... I saw someone shoot a man. He was kneeling. Kneeling with the back of his head to me, like you are now. On a carpet like you. In his house. The man who killed him, he held a gun at his side, casually, like you are now. No weight in it. No... Just his hand, natural as anything. Like a stopped pendulum. Then he just swung it up, swung it up as if it had no meaning. Swung it like an arc needs an apex, and at the height of the swing he let it take the top of the man's head off. As if the two were unconnected. As if it was simple displacement. I watched. I watched like I watch every night as the top of the man's head dissipates. I watch as the body falls to the floor and every time – every time – I think the body is going to put a hand out. Arrest it. Because. That's what bodies do. That's what we've seen them do a thousand times. They put a hand out. When they fall, they put a hand out! And that's how you tell when someone is dead. That's how you gauge it. You know they're dead if they can't be bothered to save themselves. I watched that man. I watched you. Doing that. Every night. Like I watched that boy die. Like I watched your woman die. And all I can think is how much better for everyone, how much better... If he had just let the arc continue and... A dead man never tries to stop himself...

DIARMEN RAISES THE GUN, AND IN ONE FLU-ID MOVEMENT SHOOTS HIMSELF.

AS HE DOES WE SMASH TO BLACKOUT.

END OF ACT 2.

ACT 3

ACT 3

SCENE 1

THE SITTING ROOM.

MOMENTS BEFORE SENUR HAS BEEN UN-TIED, THE ROPES STILL STREWN AROUND THE CHAIR. SENUR IS SITTING ON THE SOFA WATCHING THE DOCTOR AS HE ATTENDS TO THE WOUNDS ON HER HANDS.

HE HAS OBVIOUSLY JUST FREED HER.

THE BODIES OF THE TWO MEN HAVE BEEN RE-MOVED.

DOCTOR   Does that hurt?

SENUR   It's fine.

DOCTOR   It's lucky they... You could have been tied like that for days.

SENUR WATCHES HIM, TOUCHED BY HIS KIND-NESS.

THE DOCTOR SEES AN OLD MARK ON HER ARM AND STOPS. SHE DOESN'T PULL AWAY

DOCTOR   When was this?

SENUR   It's very old.

DOCTOR   It was well cut. We see a lot of these. With young people. In the hospitals. We see a lot of these. Young women who have... You knew what you were doing. Most people... We usually only see these on dead people.

SENUR   Have you ever been to a maze, doctor?

DOCTOR   Of course.

SENUR   One of those high... I went to one, once. A boy where I work... He was kind and... I think he thought it would be fun. Perhaps I was to lean on him. Perhaps that was the point of it. Silly girl being led by her gallant knight to safety.

DOCTOR   I have trouble seeing you in that role.

SENUR   So did I. The hedges were... It was new. That's what it said anyway, but the hedges were high, too high to see over and... Whoever built it had a very good mind, because you'd turn and turn but no matter what you did, you'd find yourself blocked. Even if you went back on yourself, you'd find your way blocked. And eventually, eventually you just wanted to rip through a wall. Just rip through it. Cheat. Climb over it or... That's what it's like to be a girl. Young. Eventually you just get tired of being blocked. I wouldn't worry about it.

PAUSE.

I suppose... With older mazes it gets easier to find your way around. You simply follow the most worn... I suppose you wish I'd succeeded.

DOCTOR   Why would you say that?

SENUR   I killed three of your friends today.

DOCTOR   Tied to a chair? No, I'm not glad you didn't succeed. I'm a doctor. We take vows.

SENUR   You are the family doctor?

DOCTOR   I gave birth to the boy. His mother – stepmother – as well.

SENUR   Was he his son? The bodyguard?

DOCTOR   Why would you say that? There that will hold. For now.

SENUR   What will happen to me?

DOCTOR   (PAUSE) You'll go to prison. I'm sorry but… The police know you are here. There will be a trial of course but….

SENUR   It won't end.

DOCTOR   It never does. Life. (PAUSE) Why did you think he was Diarmen's son? The bodyguard's?

SENUR   I thought maybe...

DOCTOR   There's a lot you don't know. About us. About this family. You should know it. All of it. For what you've done here.

SENUR   It's not important.

DOCTOR   It's impossible, you know. To judge someone. To know someone. And yet that's what we do. Doctors. Judges. We never truly know and yet we have to get on with it anyway. Diarmen... He was in love with Sarah. Always in love with her. They knew each other, went to school together. But… They were separated, as young people. Lovers, I presume. They were separated by the war. I don't know the details, but they lost contact. Perhaps they couldn't... When the judge met Sarah, he'd never met Diamen. Not then. Not until a few years ago. The... Kars was already three when he married Sarah. I delivered him myself. This was his first wife. At the beginning of the... troubles. The judge had...

SENUR   You're wrong.

DOCTOR   I'm not.

SENUR   They knew each other! The bodyguard! During the war!

DOCTOR   No. The judge was overseas when the baby came. The embargo... He wasn't supposed to be but... There were complications and... She died. In this house. So when he met Sarah....

SENUR   They knew each other!

DOCTOR   Any...No! Diarmen. The judge. He'd never even met Sarah before. Anyway, a few years after this. After the war. The judge is hiring. All departments. Let me finish! He's been put in charge of reforming the judicial sector, and that makes enemies. There was an attempt on his life. In the courthouse. So, they hire protection. Not even the judge, this is all done for him. And who do they hire but Diarmen! The one who got away! The lovers separated by war! It was all just coincidence. They'd each thought the other dead. Nothing more.

SENUR   You're wrong.

DOCTOR   I'm really not.

SENUR   You are!

DOCTOR   Why? Tell... Tell me why it matters? Because you feel responsible? Because you think killed a man whose only crime was being in love? You didn't. I saw the bodies. I saw the...(HE POINTS AT THE RESULTS OF THE SHOTGUN BLAST)

Whatever you think, whatever you... did. Today. You were not responsible. Not for that. It's not only girls who can't find the way out.

SENUR   They knew each other. Years before. During the war! The judge!

DOCTOR   No.

SENUR   They did.

DOCTOR   Senur...

SENUR   Before. In the war!

DOCTOR   I promise you...

SENUR   One night... One night. They! The judge. His bodyguard! They came to the house of a man. They came to the house of a man and killed him! There on the floor, while his family watched. They killed him! Shot him in the head and moved on. I know this!

DOCTOR   No.

SENUR   I saw it!

DOCTOR   I know. I know. I know who you are, and I'm telling you you're wrong!

SILENCE.

DOCTOR (cont) Not at first. I'll admit it. Not at first but I recognized...

SENUR   How could you?

DOCTOR   Revenge is rarely...

SENUR   This isn't revenge!

DOCTOR   No? What is it, then?

SENUR   This is justice! A murderer...

DOCTOR   Sarah – the judge's wife – didn't murder...

SENUR   She was an accident!

DOCTOR   And the boy?

SENUR   (PAUSE) I wanted him to suffer. I wanted... My father was killed right in front of me! I wanted... Justice. An eye for an eye. I wanted him to regret me. I wanted him to remember me. Forever. I wanted him to remember wanting me forever! How it felt to be inside the woman who killed his... Like that man was inside me! In my mind. Every night!

DOCTOR   No one was... You weren't even there. You were just a child.

SENUR   In my mind. In my dreams, every night! Everything! That is the punishment. That is the crime! A young girl! Her father killed in front of her... I don't care what you say! That man...

DOCTOR   He wasn't there.

SENUR   I remember him!

DOCTOR   I know. I can see that. But he wasn't there. To my knowledge he wasn't even in the country. I promise you.

SENUR   It was justice. Life for life! Destruction of destruction!

DOCTOR   No.

SENUR   How can be so sure?

DOCTOR   You... So little. I remember you. Sitting there. On the floor. When ... I haven't thought about that night in… Well, I guess twenty years.

SILENCE.

DOCTOR   Are you going to kill me now? I wouldn't mind. (PAUSE) Well, I would. But if it was someone...

SENUR   I don't believe you.

DOCTOR   It was the only thing to do. Believe me.

SILENCE.

SHE LOOKS AT HIM.

SENUR   I'm not going to kill you.

DOCTOR   Well then. (RISING) I'm sorry. For all this. I shouldn't have…

SILENCE.

DOCTOR (cont)   The police will be here in... You could escape, I suppose. I suppose... There's no one to stop you. Still...

HE GOES TO THE DOOR.

DOCTOR   What was your real name? It was... I know it's not Senur... I just can't... She… Well, I suppose it doesn't matter.

THE DOCTOR NODS AND EXITS.

SENUR SITS SILENTLY FOR A WHILE AND THEN GETS UP, GOES TO THE FRENCH DOORS AND OPENS THEM ONTO THE BALCONY. SHE STEPS OUT AND CLIMBS ONTO THE RAILING, CONTEMPLATING JUMPING.

SHE STAYS LIKE THAT FOR A MOMENT. THE JUDGE ENTERS, HIS ARM IN A SLING. HE LOOKS

TIRED AND DRAWN. HE GOES AND POURS HIMSELF A DRINK BEFORE ADDRESSING HER.

JUDGE   I'd appreciate it. If you're going to jump, I'd appreciate it.

SHE IS SURPRISED TO HEAR HIS VOICE AND HAS TO CATCH HERSELF.

JUDGE (cont) It would make things so much cleaner. I'd push you myself but I think the more distance between my arm and your teeth the better.

SENUR   I'm not going to hurt you.

JUDGE   My son is dead. So… (PAUSE) Drink?

HE HOLDS OUT A GLASS. SHE COMES DOWN OFF THE VERANDA AND LOOKS AT HIM. HE PLACES IT ON THE TABLE AND STEPS AWAY. SHE APPROACHES IT LIKE AN ANIMAL.

JUDGE (cont)   You are supposed to love your children, you know that? It's one of those preordained things. Like sunrises. The dirty secret most of us carry is we wouldn't even invite them to a dinner party if we didn't have to. Ignore me. I'm in shock. Or something I suppose. Why is my son dead?

SENUR   He tried to shoot me.

JUDGE   Why?

SENUR   He… slept with me.

JUDGE   With you?

SENUR   I slept with him. Before. At the party.

JUDGE   I see. I'm obviously in the wrong rooms at my own parties. I'll ask again. My wife. The man who loved her. I have mixed feelings about that, but my son? My son! What had he ever done to you?

SENUR   You killed my father.

JUDGE   Yes. Yes, the doctor explained everything. At the hospital. He thought he recognized you. Still, I suppose I see the... Juxtaposition. In your head at least.

SENUR   Every day... Every day!

JUDGE   Yes, I know. I said I understood. (HE SIGHS) There was this woman. In court. In court you understand, everything is heightened, everything is... She was... I don't remember what she was there for. What she was doing there. I don't even remember what I said to her. It was... Something snide no doubt. Something challenging. To me, nothing. But to her.... Anyway, she... First there were letters. From her. Then letters to the papers. Again it was never truly clear what I had done but... (PAUSE) When I was a boy my father would never allow me in his library. Never allowed in there. First thing I did when he died... I went into the library and burnt his books. Not the same I suppose. You'll have to excuse me. The painkillers.

SENUR   My father was a good man.

JUDGE   I'm sure he was.

SENUR   And you killed him.

JUDGE   We did. Yes. It wasn't personal. You know, the worst of them... I've had people through my courts. Really bad people. People who have committed... Child molesters. Rapists! People who have killed... And each and every one of them has had someone, someone who will stand up in court and tell you what a good person they are. Deep down. If nothing else we've become incredibly apt at fooling people.

SENUR   Like you, you mean?

JUDGE   Probably. And this was nothing to do with the senator? No night of the generals?

SENUR   Would you be alive if it were?

JUDGE   No. No. I suppose not. I am, it seems, an old woman in a court house. Shouting.

SENUR   When you shot my father...

JUDGE   When you shot my wife!

SENUR   When you shoot me!

THE JUDGE PULLS A GUN OUT OF HIS SLING.

JUDGE   This? Yes. I'm not sure. It was Diarmen's. The one I suppose... The doctor has promised to leave us alone. Until the police get here.

HE PUTS THE GUN DOWN ON THE TABLE AND POURS HIMSELF A DRINK. SENUR EYES THE GUN CAREFULLY.

JUDGE (cont) He was a good man. Diarmen. A good counsellor. One cannot legislate the heart. I've tried. Or fate come to that. You can't legislate it. The doctor tells me you think tonight... Justice.

SENUR   I thought he was there.

JUDGE   Diarmen?

SENUR   The night you...

JUDGE   You thought he was with me?

SENUR   I thought that's why...

JUDGE   Why he killed himself? He did kill himself, I take it. You don't seem the type for... No... Yes. We'll never know, I suppose. Not really. But I'd guess it had something to do with honour. It usually does. Honour and love.

SENUR   How could you put up with…

JUDGE   The betrayal? No. People are more complicated than that. Much more. (PAUSE) I'd like to tell you about your father. If that's alright with you? I don't mean… Maybe we'll wrestle for the gun. Maybe I'll get tired and just shoot you. Maybe you'll shoot me. But I'd like to. Tell you. About your father. If it's something you want.

SILENCE.

JUDGE (cont)   Your father had a sister. I don't know if he ever... No. Well, I didn't know him. Not even of him. He wasn't from here. Not originally. But I suppose you know that. I wondered, at the time, why he stayed here. Why not just... leave. I don't suppose you'd tell me? No? No, I doubt you even know. Not really. (PAUSE) We lost ten thousand that first year. That's what ethnic cleansing does. What it's like. There is no hatred more natural than for those not like us. And we knew why. We knew the catalyst. But a... A friend. Of your father's... You are too young to remember the war. Not really. And it wasn't the best way, but it had to be done. And if I had to do it all over again.... There are times when justice has to be dragged into the street, and there are times it's better behind closed… (HE DRINKS) People kill people. Not ideals or money. People. And we will do it for the slightest excuse. I think it scares us. Life. I think we can't look at it properly. So big and so vast. Endless from our perspective. So we create… Laws. Reasons. God's and man's. Put us on one side of it and others on another and ask everyone to… get along. There are more cock-eyed ways of punishing a person than there are of anything else. I'm old. And stupid. And maybe I was wrong. But we'd barely started to get it stopped when we found out it was your father. (HE DRINKS AGAIN, EXHAUSTED) I'm tired. I think. They gave me something for the pain. I said I'd shoot you if I was tired, didn't I? Still. (HE PAUSES) I think I'll go to bed instead.

HE RISES. SHE ALMOST MOVES TO HELP HIM.

JUDGE (cont) Be so good as to wait here for the police, would you.

HE GOES TO THE DOOR.

JUDGE (cont) I miss my son. (PAUSE) Will that be enough, do you think?

SILENCE.

JUDGE (cont) Good night, child.

HE EXITS. SHE SITS THERE, THE GUN NEAR HER. WE WAIT. LIGHTS START TO FADE. WE SEE THE FLASH OF POLICE LIGHTS. SHE REMAINS STILL.

FADE TO BLACKOUT.

END OF SCENE 1.

SCENE 2

THE JUDGE'S OFFICE AT THE LAW COURTS

DAYS LATER.

THE JUDGE HAS JUST RETURNED TO HIS OFFICE FROM COURT. PAPERS ARE STREWN ACROSS HIS DESK. HE SLOWLY SLIDES HIS ROBE OFF, CAREFUL OF HIS STILL PAINFUL SHOULDER, AND HANGS IT UP.

THERE IS A KNOCK AT THE DOOR.

JUDGE   Come.

THE DOOR OPENS AND SENATOR MATGOLISE ENTERS.

SENATOR There was no one outside.

JUDGE   Come in. No, no one outside. I didn't think either of us wanted any chance of this conversation being overheard, senator.

SENATOR I see. I was sorry to hear about your son. Your wife too, of course.

JUDGE   Thank you.

SENATOR Such terrible times we live in. In your own home, too. Just... shocking!

JUDGE   Have a seat senator.

SENATOR It's a good thing I wasn't invited. To the party, I mean. I shudder to think....

JUDGE   I wanted this chance to talk.

SENATOR   I'm guessing this isn't about judicial overview, then.

JUDGE   No. And I'm sorry about the subterfuge.

SENATOR   She was an ex-convict, I hear. The assassin. An ex-convict. A... custodian of these courts.

JUDGE   No. No, she wasn't.

SENATOR   Is that right? Well. Guess we can't believe what we read in the papers these days after all.

JUDGE   I suppose not.

SENATOR   I'm just saying. Nothing you hear or see is the truth.

JUDGE   Isn't it?

SENATOR   I'd believe you know that better than anyone... Judge. I'm just saying, because if I've been dragged in here for a scolding. I...

JUDGE   A scolding?

SENATOR Out of respect for your family...

JUDGE   A scolding? Senator. I'm not sure...

SENATOR   I was hoping you were calling me down to build bridge....

JUDGE   Khadife Sedat. It helps to say her name out loud.

SENATOR   Be careful what you're insinuating, judge.

JUDGE   I'm insinuating that you raped and killed Khadife Sedat. I'm insinuating that you invited her to your home. I don't care why. And that when she tried to leave, you forcibly raped her and strangled her in your own living room.

SENATOR   Out of deference to the dead...

JUDGE   Fuck the dead. I'm insinuating that you bribed police officials. Made or helped make evidence disappear, and put pressure on the newspapers to cover it up.

SENATOR (RISING) If that's all you...

JUDGE   Sit! Down! (BEAT) Didn't matter to you that she was a child. Maybe that helped. I'm not one to judge. No, wait. That's exactly what I am! It didn't matter that she was a child! It didn't matter that she was poor, uneducated...

SENATOR   Well! I would think you of all people...

JUDGE.   I of all people would... What?

SENATOR   Didn't you just have your own little run in with a native girl?

PAUSE.

JUDGE   Senator, do you know what the party was for the night of...

SENATOR   I know I wasn't invited.

JUDGE   No. No, it was a party to see if I still held any sway. To see if I still had any clout. Enough to take you down. Police, press, decision makers... I wanted to know just how many you had in your back pocket.

SENATOR   And how'd that go for you?

JUDGE   This country hangs by a thread. A literal thread!

SENATOR   What's it made of – horse shit?

JUDGE   Justice! I've always believed that. If justice can be done... If justice can be seen to be done then...

SENATOR Like I said. Horse shit!

JUDGE   We lost... thousands. In the war. Tens of thousands. Both sides. The sheer...

SENATOR   We'll agree to disagree on that.

JUDGE   The numbers?

SENATOR   The loss!

SILENCE.

JUDGE   I want you to resign senator.

SENATOR   No.

JUDGE   Just like that?

SENATOR   Just like that.

JUDGE   The ease with which this country...

SENATOR   Let it. Let it! They want rid of us? We want rid of them. I like our odds! Justice? Whose justice? Ours? Theirs? You don't have it, judge. You don't have it! And even if you did, you wouldn't use it! You said so yourself. This country hangs by a thread. How'd justice go for us last time? How'd it solve our ills, huh? You don't have it! I'm staying! I'm staying, and I don't want you to be alarmed but I think we are going to have to take a look at that judicial practices thing again. These lifetime appointments... I don't know! People don't want justice, judge. They just don't! What we don't know can't hurt us. Ain't that the saying? All this begating... Well, it just ain't good for the soul, now is it? Violence needs violence! And what we don't know... Well, that's just the way of the world. Justice begats justice, judge. We want peace, we're just gonna have to renounce justice.

HE RISES TO EXIT.

SENATOR I really am sorry about your boy. A tragedy. Truly. And after that... Well, I just don't know if I could carry on. You?

HE EXITS. LIGHTS DOWN ON THE JUDGE AS HE FADES AWAY.

END OF SCENE 2.

SCENE 3

AN OLD HOUSE ON THE OUTSKIRTS OF THE CITY. TWENTY YEARS BEFORE.

A SMALL GIRL – SENUR AS A CHILD – IS PLAYING IN FRONT OF HER FATHER, KIFUR, WHO IS ASLEEP IN AN ARM CHAIR.

OBVIOUSLY POOR, SHE IS PLAYING WITH A SOLITARY DOLL. SHE TWISTS THE DOLL AND AN ARM COMES OFF.

SHE TURNS TO HER FATHER.

YOUNG SENUR   Pappy.... Pappy...

KIFUR   What is it Senur?

YOUNG SENUR   I think Antolia is in trouble.

KIFUR   Is that right, darling?

YOUNG SENUR Her arm's come off.

KIFUR   That is unfortunate.

YOUNG SENUR   She'll need fixing.

KIFUR   I expect she will.

UNSEEN TO KIFUR BUT OBVIOUS TO THE GIRL, THE JUDGE AND THE DOCTOR ENTER, BOTH WRAPPED IN LARGE OVERCOATS. THIS IS MANY YEARS AGO, AND BOTH MEN SEEM YOUNGER.

SENUR   Pappy!

DOCTOR   Kifur.

KIFUR RISES. HE ALMOST SEEMS TO BE EXPECTING THE TWO MEN. THE JUDGE LOOKS AROUND DISAPPROVINGLY, STAMPING OFF THE COLD.

KIFUR   Hello doctor.

DOCTOR   How have you been, Kifur?

KIFUR   This and that.

JUDGE   We need to talk.

DOCTOR   This is judge Alenvardos. He's... Well, we have a few questions for you.

KIFUR   My daughter is here.

JUDGE   I'll look after her.

SENUR   Pappy?

KIFUR   It's all right. Senur. Stay here.

THE DOCTOR AND KIFUR STEP AWAY TO TALK.

JUDGE   Hello.

SENUR   Hello.

DOCTOR   We'll just go over here.

Thomas Alexander

JUDGE   And who is this?

SENUR   Antolia. Her arm's come off.

JUDGE   She looks like she's been in the wars.

SENUR NODS.

JUDGE (cont) Can I see her?

SHE HANDS THE DOLL OVER AND HE LOOKS
FOR A WAY TO REATTACH THE ARM.

JUDGE (cont)   Do you know the story of toys?
No? Well, I'll tell you! Toys are built with the big-
gest hearts. In fact, that's all they are. Hearts. You
know what hearts are? Well, the problem with big
hearts is that the bigger the heart is, the more precognisant they are. Do you know what that means?
Precognisant? No? Well, you know when you can
tell weather is coming, or... You are thinking about
someone and then suddenly there they are, right in
front of you! Yes? Well, it's like that. They can see the
future. We only have little hearts, in proportion, so
we can only see things a little way off. But toys, they
are all heart. So every toy, from the moment they
are made, they can see the future. Their future. All
of it. They see when you buy them. They see when
they come home with you, what kind of home it is,
and they see you growing. Changing. They see when
they're important to you, and they see the day when
you are just too big to play with them anymore. They
even see the years of being stored away in boxes, or...
Thrown away and... This is the thing with toys. With
precognition. They can choose, whether they want
to be with you! Whether they want to be with you or
wait for another child to come into the store. By the
look of Antolia she must love you very much.

DOCTOR   Judge?

THE JUDGE RISES AND JOINS THE TWO MEN. YOUNG SENUR STAYS WITH ANATOLIA.

THE DOCTOR NODS AS HE APPROACHES.

KIFUR   It was me.

JUDGE   Just like that?

KIFUR   I'm not sorry for it.

DOCTOR   Kifur...

JUDGE   You're not sorry?

KIFUR   It's their law!

JUDGE   Their...

DOCTOR   He says she was alive when he left her.

JUDGE   Their law! You... You raped a pregnant woman. Raped and hung.

DOCTOR   He's saying she wasn't dead.

KIFUR   I didn't know she was pregnant!

JUDGE   And that...

DOCTOR   Keep your voice down!

JUDGE   You've... You've seen what's happening? In the papers? Out there! The bloodshed!

KIFUR   They killed my sister. Burnt her alive while she knelt in prayer.

DOCTOR   They were...

JUDGE   The... Damn you! That was...

KIFUR   My sister was a righteous woman!

JUDGE   It was a mistake. A mistake! There had

been... As soon as they knew...

KIFUR   It was not a mistake. They set fire to the...

JUDGE   They set fire to the building because it was built on their lands! Ceremonial lands! They didn't know... your beliefs.

KIFUR   Did they turn themselves in? Once they realised? Did they throw themselves on the mercy of your courts?

JUDGE   They wouldn't have made it a day! They'd have been lynched!

KIFUR   Their justice. Not mine. There's... There's not a... I'm ready to pay my price.

DOCTOR   I think we can...

JUDGE   It's genocide. Do you know that? Estimates are in the thousands. By the end of the month, there won't be any... The courts are flooded.

KIFUR   They killed my sister. In prayer. I did not make their justice. I simply carried it out.

DOCTOR   He's saying he didn't kill her.

KIFUR   It was within the law.

SILENCE.

KIFUR   I know what has to be done.

THE JUDGE PULLS A PISTOL OUT OF HIS COAT AND LETS IT HANG AT HIS SIDE.

DOCTOR   Not here!

JUDGE   Where then? You'd take him into the capital? The court? Which court? It'd be on fire by morning. No. No one can know about this. I'm sorry. But no one can know! What happened… If we're going to have any chance of putting a lid on this thing… What happened… It's a myth. Fiction! You can't put a fire out with petrol. I'm sorry.

DOCTOR   I thought… I though justice done in secret couldn't be justice!

JUDGE   That's just something we tell people!

KIFUR   I don't regret what I did.

JUDGE   Then neither will I. Take the girl out front.

KIFUR   She has family. Across the border. With our people. They will look after her.

JUDGE   She'll be well taken care of, I promise. Take her out front.

DOCTOR   No! I…

KIFUR   Please. While my courage stands!

DOCTOR   Me. It should be me. My… Ilsa. It should be me.

KIFUR   Swear she'll be taken care of!

THE JUDGE HESITATES AND THEN HANDS THE DOCTOR THE GUN.

JUDGE   I promise

KIFUR TURNS AND KNEELS.

KIFUR   Quickly.

THE JUDGE TURNS AND SCOOPS YOUNG SENUR UP INTO HIS ARMS, HEADING FOR THE DOOR. THE CHILD CRIES OUT FOR HER DOLL.

YOUNG SENUR   Anatolia! Anatolia! No! Pappy!

THE JUDGE EXITS, HER ARMS AND FACE STREAMING OVER HIS SHOULDER INTO THE HOVEL.

DOCTOR   By the power invested...

KIFUR   No words. Just do it. If you're going to...

SILENCE. THE DOCTOR SEEMS HESITANT. THE GUN PRESSED AGAINST THE SIDE OF THE MAN'S TEMPLE.

KIFUR   Do you even know how...

THE GUN GOES OFF. KIFUR FALLS DEAD AS WE SMASH TO BLACKOUT.

CURTAINS.

END

Also by

THOMAS ALEXANDER

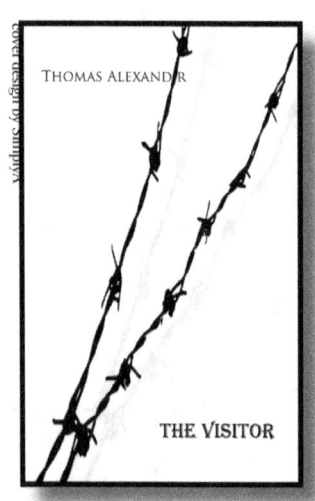

THOMAS ALEXANDER

THE VISITOR

THE VISITOR

BY

THOMAS ALEXANDER

WHEN THE LOVER OF A FAMOUS WRITER GOES MISSING IN A WAR RAVAGED COUNTRY, HE BRIBES HIS WAY INTO A JAIL TO QUESTION HER HUSBAND, A MISSIONARY, WHO IS BEING TORTURED AS A TRAINING EXERCISE BY HIS CAPTORS.

ALONE IN THE CELL, THE TWO START A DIALOGUE ABOUT THE NATURE OF BELIEF.

BELIEF IN GOD, LOVE AND POLITICS.

MURDER ME GENTLY

By

Thomas Alexander

*"ONE MAN... ONE WOMAN...
AND THE QUEST FOR JUSTICE
IN AN UNJUST WORLD"*

MODERN DAY RUSSIA
THROUGH THE MEDIUM OF
FILM NOIR

BLENDING REAL LIFE EVENTS WITH COMEDY AND INTRIGUE, *MURDER ME GENTLY'S* UNIQUE PERSPECTIVE ON THE WORLD OF RUSSIAN POLITICS AS SEEN THROUGH THE LENS OF FILM NOIR, SPANS THE ASSASSINATION OF INTERNATIONALLY RENOWNED JOURNALISTS, PUTIN'S REACH FOR THE RETURN OF SOVIET SATELLITE STATES, AND THE INFILTRATION OF GOVERNMENT BY OLIGARCHS AND CRIMINALS.

PROVIDING A DAMMING INDICTMENT OF THE WEST'S INABILITY TO HALT MOSCOW'S POLICY OF EXPANSIONISM *MURDER ME GENTLY* LENDS A THEATRICAL EXPOSE TO THE VERY REAL WORLD OF CORRUPTION AND GREED IN INTERNATIONAL POLITICS TODAY.

*A CONMAN, A DISGRACED INTERPOL AGENT, A MA-
FIA BOSS, A CIA SPOOK, AND THE SECRET TO THE
FUTURE ALL UNITE IN AN UNLIKELY ALLIANCE IN A
LOVE AFFAIR THAT WILL DEFINE THE FATE OF THE
WORLD IN* THOMAS ALEXANDER'S

... MURDER ME ... GENTLY!

GREAT

BY

THOMAS ALEXANDER

A REMOTE ROOM IN THE THROWS OF WINTER.

THE ONCE GREAT MAN LIVES ALONE NOW WITH HIS SON,

AN OLD FRIEND HAS COME TO VISIT. HE HAS CLIMBED UP FROM THE VILLAGE IN ORDER TO OFFER THE OLD MAN ONE LAST CHANCE TO ESCAPE THE ENCROACHING WINTER THAT IS ABOUT TO TAKE HIM, STIRRING UP MEMORIES OF BETTER TIMES AND THE WARMTH OF SUMMER.

BEGAT

BY

THOMAS ALEXANDER

IN A COUNTRY, AFTER THE WAR, A JUDGE THROWS A DINNER PARTY, SEEKING SUPPORT AGAINST A POWERFUL MINISTER WHO HAS RAPED AND KILLED A SERVANT GIRL.

BUT THE JUDGE HIMSELF IS THE TARGET TONIGHT, AND THE SHADOW OF THE WAR HE SO DESPERATELY WANTS TO LEAVE BEHIND THREATENS TO ENGULF HIS FAMILY AS A YOUNG WOMAN SEEKS REVENGE FOR THE SINS OF HIS PAST.

Happiness

By

Thomas Alexander

On a remote headland in North Wales a man and his paraplegic son dream of life beyond the confines of their four walls.

But when a woman offers them the escape they so crave they find they are bound by more then their dreams.

The jealousy of a bored policeman and the kindness of a mail order bride set them on a path of hope and destruction.

THE LAST CHRISTMAS

BY

THOMAS ALEXANDER

WHEN AN EMBATTLED NEWSROOM RECEIVES A POTENTIALLY EARTH SHATTERING STORY MINUTES BEFORE AIR ON CHRISTMAS DAY THE CAREFUL EQUILIBRIUM OF THE TEAM IS SHATTERED AND OLD DIVIDING LINES COME TO THE FORE, TURNING CO-WORKER AGAINST CO-WORKER.

SET IN REAL TIME AND INCORPORATING ACTUAL AND INTERCHANGEABLE NEWS EVENTS THE LAST CHRISTMAS PITS SOCIAL POLITICS AGAINST JOURNALISTIC INTEGRITY IN A BATTLE OF THE ETHICS.

GOD

By

THOMAS ALEXANDER

WHEN THE NAMED PARTNER OF A SMALL LAW FIRM DIES, LEAVING LARGE DEBT, THE REMAINING MISFITS OF THE FIRM ARE FORCED TO TAKE ON JUST ABOUT ANY CLIENT AVAILABLE, INCLUDING A LITIGIOUS SOCCER-MUM WHO WOULD LIKE TO SUE GOD FOR THE DEATH OF HER HUSBAND – HIT BY A LIGHTNING BOLT ON THE 15TH HOLE OF A MUNICIPAL GOLF COURSE.

THE TRIAL BECOMES COMPLICATED HOWEVER, WHEN AN INDIGENT WITH NO BACKGROUND AND A CANNY KNACK OF KNOWING EVERYONE'S BACKGROUND ENTERS THE COURTROOM CLAIMING TO BE 'GOD'.

BATTING BACK AND FORE BETWEEN THE COURTROOM AND THE PERSONAL LIVES OF THE LAWYERS, 'GOD' IS A FAST PACED COURTROOM DRAMA/COMEDY THAT USES ORIGINAL STAGING AND NON-LINEAR STORYTELLING TO PROVIDE A LIGHT-HEARTED, BUT COMPLEX SOCIAL DRAMA.

THE FAMILY

BY

THOMAS ALEXANDER

TODAY, FOR THE FIRST TIME IN LONGER THAN ANYONE CAN REMEMBER, THE FAMILY ARE GATHERING. THEY ARE GATHERING TO CELE- BRATE THE ENGAGEMENT OF THE MATRIARCHAL NIECE, THEY ARE GATHERING TO CELEBRATE THE LAST BIRTHDAY OF THE PATRIARCH, THEY ARE GATHERING TO WELCOME HOME THE PRODI- GAL SON AND HIS BEAUTIFUL GIRLFRIEND AND THEY ARE GOING TO CELEBRATE ALL THIS WITH A SLIDESHOW.

CANDID PHOTOGRAPHS. PHOTOGRAPHS OF THINGS NO ONE THOUGHT ANYONE ELSE KNEW ABOUT. PHOTOGRAPH TAKEN WHEN NO ONE ELSE WAS THERE.

IT'S ALL COMING OUT TODAY. IN BLACK AND WHITE FOR EVERYONE TO SEE. THE REMNANTS OF CHILD ABUSE, INFIDELITY, LOSS, DESTRUC- TION AND MISSED BIRTHDAY PARTIES. IT'S ALL COMING OUT. IT'S GOING TO BE A LONG NIGHT. POSSIBLY FOREVER.

THE RECRUITMENT OFFICER

BY

THOMAS ALEXANDER

TOM, A CHARMING YANKEE RECRUITER, COMES TO AN UNSPECIFIED ENGLISH TOWN AND FALLS IN LOVE WITH THE CONFERENCE CENTRE MANAGER, JULIA.

BUT WHAT EXACTLY IS HE RECRUITING FOR? WHY DOES EVERYONE WHO JOINS NEVER COME BACK AND WHAT IS ON THE OTHER SIDE OF THE DOOR

WHERE DO THE RECRUITS GO AFTER SIGNING UP?

AN EXISTENTIAL LOVE STORY THAT ASKS QUESTIONS OF WHO WE ARE, WHAT WE WANT FROM LIFE AND WHETHER WE'RE GETTING IT, THE RECRUITMENT OFFICER IS A REMODELLING OF THE 1706 PLAY BY GEORGE FARQUHAR. *THE RECRUITING OFFICER*

Writer's Block

By

Thomas Alexander

Paul Block was once a prolific writer. A recipient of both the Pen and Faulkner-awards and the author of over ten different novels, he was once considered the UK's most up and coming writer until, at the age of forty, he suffered a nervous breakdown.

Ten years later the world has forgotten Paul Block. Holed up in his study he has been working on the same first page of his new novel for nearly five years, kept company by only his maid, a foul mouthed Irish hit-man, a veteran of the battle of Gettysburg and a nineteen forties femme fetal.

Today, all that's going to change. Paul has a busy day ahead of him. First he's going to kill a persistent and charmless young reporter who wants to do a piece on 'Writer's block' and then he's going to have a rare visit from his son who's bringing him bad news and a new couch.

With a missing body and a son who hates him, Paul must finally rid himself of his protagonists if he's ever going to stay out of jail, and finish that first page.

WRITING WILLIAM
BY
THOMAS ALEXANDER

"We want to put our education to use and our education is, was, and god damned always will be William fucking Shakespeare! We want lines we don't understand. We want plot holes so big you can drive a truck through them! We want to make sense of it all! Or at least understand what we studied it for in the first place! You want to put on a play? We want Shakespeare!"

Released in commemoration of Shakespeare's 450th anniversary this special edition of Writing William contains the original playbill and deleted scenes along with a new forward by Thomas Alexander.

Writing William follows a young, aspiring, playwright who, in order to get his work on stage, forges a Shakespeare play.

Basing the play on the relationship between Henry II and Eleanor of Aquitaine during the murder of Thomas Becket, Will, starts to see it mirror his own failing marriage as he struggles to find approval from an unforgiving spouse.

Backed by a working class billionaire and supported by an array of aging actors, the lead of which is mute, Will finds cathartic release in the writing of the play and it's impending production, but he hasn't taken into account just how gullible the theatre going public truly are.

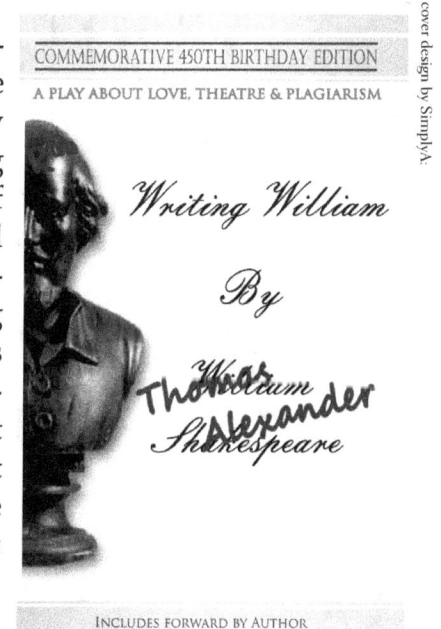

COMMEMORATIVE 450TH BIRTHDAY EDITION

A PLAY ABOUT LOVE, THEATRE & PLAGIARISM

Writing William

By

Thomas William Shakespeare Alexander

INCLUDES FORWARD BY AUTHOR
DELETED SCENES & ORIGINAL PLAYBILL

A comedic farce, Writing William blends Shakespearian dialogue with modern humour and innovative staging to look at the relationship of the artist and his art, the burden of success upon a relationship, and the true cost of producing a play.

THOMAS

Japan, 1945 – A Family At War

When a wandering priest escaping a troubled past is taken in by a prominent family, a quiet city in northern Japan is forced to confront the dark shadows of war seeping into their lives in ways they could never have anticipated.

With its townsmen scattered throughout the farthest ends of a desperate empire in a final defence against the encroaching West, the idyllic northern city of Morioka, far removed from the harsh realities of the front, is largely left to itself.

THOMAS ALEXANDER

A Scattering
of Orphans

But when a prominent doctor is conscripted and sent to Manila, his sister is left as head of the household and must deal with a young priest living at the bottom of their garden with a large collection of maps and strange knowledge of English.

As the cold hand of war approaches, each person must choose their own destiny and place in the new world.

THE OTHER SIDE

ALEXANDER

Commemorating the 70th Anniversary of the end of WW2! A trilogy spanning the length of the war from the viewpoint of an ordinary Japanese family.

Thomas Alexander

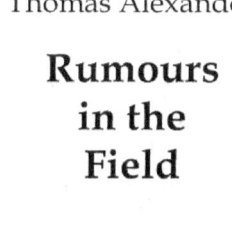

Rumours in the Field

omas Alexander

Beyond The Noonday Sun

Offering a unique perspective through the eyes of a rural Japanese family into the impact of history's bloodiest war to date, *A Scattering of Orphans* is one families attempt to make sense of a changing world amidst the desolation of war both home and abroad.

OF THE SUN